A COUNTRY FAR AWAY

STORY BY
NIGEL GRAY

PICTURES BY
PHILIPPE DUPASQUIER

Andersen Press · London

Today was just an ordinary day. I stayed at home.

I did a lot of jobs to help my mum and dad.

They were really pleased.

Today was the last day of school before the holiday.

We went home early.

I did bike riding with my friends. I'm one of the best.

My mum had a baby. We can't decide what to call her.

Today it rained – so we went swimming.

We went into town to do some shopping.

I thought we were never going to get there.

We had to get ever so many things. It was really good fun.

We had a celebration for my baby sister.

We had our photograph taken.

We played football. I scored a goal.

My cousin came to visit. We stayed up late.

I looked at some pictures of a country far away.

I'd like to go there one day . . .

. . . and make friends.

I'd like to go
to the other side of a rainbow,
far beyond the magic of its arch
to a land that would be
new and strange.

At my journey's end,
would I find someone to be my friend?
And if so,
what could he teach me?
And what could I teach him in exchange?

I've been told
it would be a long, long way.
But I will go there –
one day.